DANIEL O'ROURKE

AN IRISH TALE

Told and illustrated by GERALD McDERMOTT

Viking Kestrel

About This Book

The pooka is one of the many spirit creatures who inhabit the magical landscape
of Irish folklore. It is responsible, along with fairies and leprechauns, for much of the
capricious mischief that befalls ordinary folk. In the shape of a horse, the pooka often takes
unsuspecting humans on a wild nocturnal ride: a true "night mare."

The tale of *Daniel O'Rourke* was first collected in the early nineteenth century
in County Cork, Ireland, by T. Crofton Croker.

The artwork was rendered on illustration board in sepia ink with watercolor washes and
pastel pencil.

VIKING KESTREL

Viking Penguin Inc., 40 West 23rd Street, New York, New York 10010, U.S.A.
Penguin Books Ltd, Harmondsworth, Middlesex, England
Penguin Books Australia Ltd, Ringwood, Victoria, Australia
Penguin Books Canada Limited, 2801 John Street, Markham, Ontario, Canada L3R 1B4
Penguin Books (N.Z.) Ltd, 182–190 Wairau Road, Auckland 10, New Zealand

Copyright © Gerald McDermott, 1986
All rights reserved

First published in 1986 by Viking Penguin Inc.
Published simultaneously in Canada

Printed in Japan by Dai Nippon. Set in Sabon Roman.
1   2   3   4   5   90   89   88   87   86

Library of Congress Cataloging in Publication Data
McDermott, Gerald.   Daniel O'Rourke.
Summary: Because of a pooka spirit, Daniel O'Rourke
embarks on a fantastic journey.
[1. Folklore—Ireland]   I. Title.
PZ8.1.M159Dan   1986   398.2' 1' 09415   [E]   85-20188   ISBN 0-670-80924-1

For Marianna and Max

On a fine summer evening, many years ago, Daniel O'Rourke went up to a grand party at the great mansion on the hill.

Folks both rich and poor had been invited to join in the merriment.
There was music and laughter and plenty of food and drink.
Dan danced and danced until he could dance no more.

Then he dined on green cheese and goose livers until he thought
he would burst. It was well after midnight when he finally paid
his respects and said farewell.

Daniel O'Rourke stepped out into the night, passed through the great stone gates of the mansion, and walked down the hill toward the little white cottage where he lived with his mother. Dan paused for a moment by the pooka spirit's tower, stretched, yawned, and then continued on his way. Just as he was about to cross the brook, he looked up and saw all the stars in the summer sky.

"Lovely," he said.

It was then that he missed his footing on a slippery stone, stumbled, and fell headlong into the water. Suddenly the quiet little brook became a rushing river that sparkled like the Milky Way.

"Death Alive! I'll be drowned now!" cried Daniel.

He was swept away on a wild ride that carried him far out to sea.

After tossing about for what seemed like hours, Daniel was washed up on the misty shores of a strange island. Though the moon was bright, Daniel O'Rourke could see nothing, so he sat down on a rock and scratched his head.

Just then a black shape circled down from the sky and landed with a pounce in front of Dan. Sure but it was an eagle!

"Daniel O'Rourke," said the bird. "How do you do?"

"Very well, I thank you, sir," said Dan. "I only wish I was home again."

"Well, then, up on my back, Dan," said the eagle. "I'll take you away from this place."

Daniel O'Rourke soon found himself being carried high up into the sky. But instead of taking Dan to his mother's little white cottage, the eagle flew higher and higher until they reached the moon. There was a reaping-hook sticking out of it and the eagle dropped Dan on the end of the handle.

"Dan," said the eagle. "Hold tight to the reaping-hook, for I'll be saying goodnight to you now."

"You can't leave me here!" cried Dan.

"I can and I will," replied the eagle. "You see, Dan, I know 'twas you who robbed my nest last year. Now we're even."

The eagle flew off, laughing. Dan bawled after him, calling him a beast and a brute, but all for nothing. There Dan stayed, hanging from a hook on the moon.

Just then a door opened in the middle of the moon.

"Good morning, Daniel O'Rourke," said a little man with a long white beard. "How do you do?"

"Very well, your honor," said Dan.

"And how did you come to be here?" the little man asked.

Dan then told him the story of how he had gotten lost and been brought to the moon.

"'Tis a lovely tale, Dan," said the man in the moon. "But here you must not stay. So be off in less than no time."

"Is that any way to treat a man so far from home?" cried Dan. "You scoundrel! I'll not budge."

"We'll see how that is to be," said the little old man, and he disappeared inside.

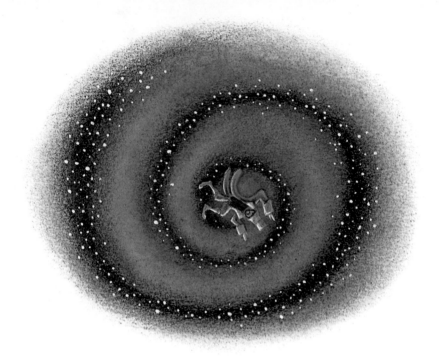

Quick as a wink the man in the moon was back with his kitchen cleaver. *Whap*! he chopped the handle of the reaping-hook in half and Daniel O'Rourke went falling through the clouds.

"Farewell to you, Dan," called the little old man. "Don't come again unless you're invited."

Daniel O'Rourke tumbled over and over, down through the night sky.

"This is a pretty pickle for a decent man to be in," said Dan as he fell.

The words were hardly out of his mouth when *whoosh*!, a flock of wild geese flew by.

The old gander who was their leader looked up and said, "Is that you, Dan?"

These geese, you see, were from a pond at the end of Dan's very own lane.

"Are you in good health this morning, Dan?"

"I'm very well, sir, thank you," said Dan, gasping for breath.

"I think 'tis falling you are, Dan," said the gander.

"Right you are, sir," replied Dan.

"Then grab hold of my leg," said the gander. "Where is it you're going so fast?"

So Dan told him the long story of how he came to be in such a fix.

"Dan, I'll save you," said the goose. "Just hold on and I'll fly you home."

They flew and they flew over the great water. Dan saw his own beloved shores and his mother's little white cottage far below him.

"Stop here!" said Dan, but they flew further still. Soon the land receded into the distance, and Dan found himself being carried over water once again.

"Please, sir, let me down," begged Dan.

"Very well," said the goose, and gave a great flap of his wings.

Dan lost his grip and went tumbling down.

He plunged into the water and sank down to the very bottom of the sea.

Just as he lost all hope, *whish*! he was shot up into the air. A great whale was bouncing him up and down on a spout of water.

When Dan was thoroughly soaked, he heard someone say, "Get up!"

It was his dear old mother, throwing a bucket of water in his face.

"Get up, Daniel!" she said. "Only a fool would fall asleep under the tower of the pooka. You've had no easy rest of it, I'm sure."

Daniel O'Rourke agreed.

Never again did he rob an eagle's nest, or eat green cheese, or dine on goose livers. And that was the last time Daniel O'Rourke slept under the pooka's tower and not in his very own bed.